# T Is for TERRIBLE

## PETER McCARTY

Henry Holt and Company

New York

I am Tyrannosaurus Rex.
I am a dinosaur,
otherwise known as
a terrible lizard.

I do not know why
I am so terrible.

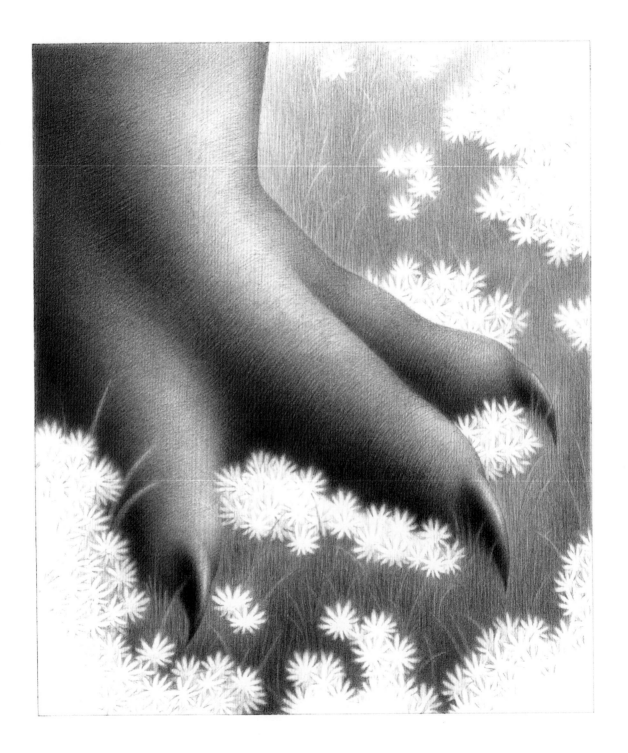

I cannot help that I step
on little flowers when I walk.

Or that the
ground shakes
when I run.

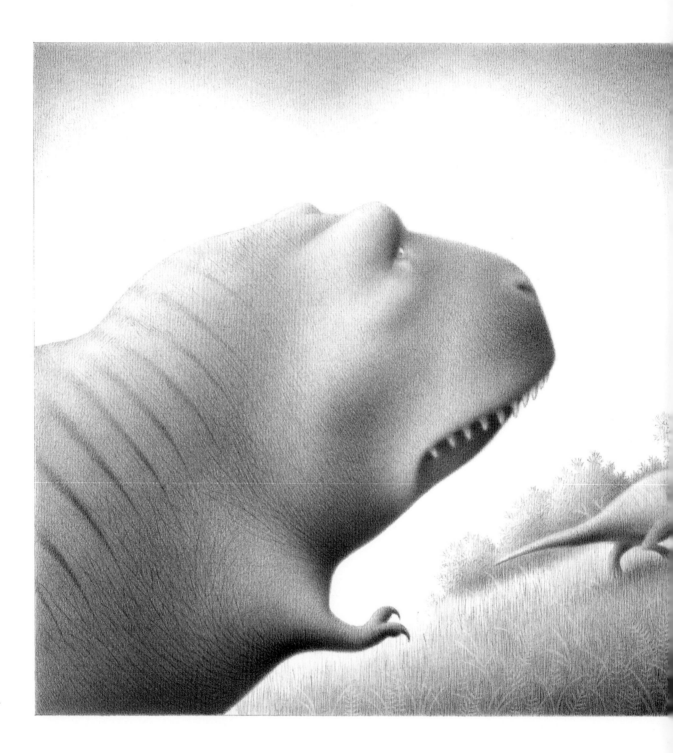

Would I be so terrible
if I were pink?

Or blue?

I am much like
other creatures.

When I was born,
I came out of an egg.

I too had a mother.

As I became older,
I grew and grew.

I cannot help
that I grew so
enormous and
so enormously
hungry.

If I could,
I would be a vegetarian.

But I am Tyrannosaurus Rex,
and I do not eat trees.

I cannot help that
I am so terrible.

# To Henry

Henry Holt and Company, LLC
*Publishers since 1866*
115 West 18th Street
New York, New York 10011
www.henryholt.com

Henry Holt is a registered trademark of Henry Holt and Company, LLC
Copyright © 2004 by Peter McCarty

Distributed in Canada by H. B. Fenn and Company Ltd.

Library of Congress Cataloging-in-Publication Data
McCarty, Peter.
T is for terrible / written and illustrated by Peter McCarty.
Summary: A tyrannosaurus rex explains that he cannot help it
that he is enormous and hungry and is not a vegetarian.
[1. Tyrannosaurus rex–Fiction. 2. Dinosaurs–Fiction.] I. Title.
PZ7.M12835 Tae    [E]–dc22    2003018246
ISBN 0-8050-7404-X / EAN 978-0-8050-7404-8 / First Edition–2004
The artist used pencil on watercolor paper
to create the illustrations for this book.
Designed by Donna Mark
Printed in the United States of America on acid-free paper. ∞
1   3   5   7   9   10   8   6   4   2